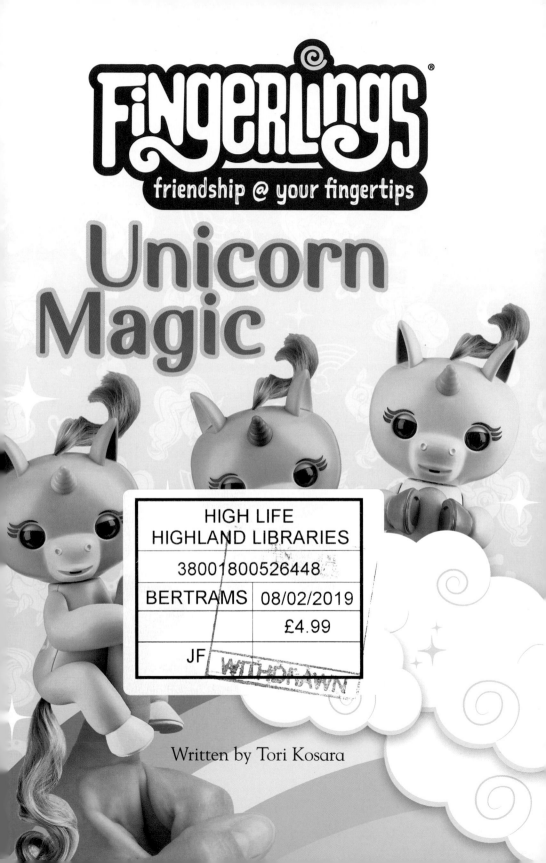

Unicorn Magic

FINGERLINGS®
friendship @ your fingertips

Written by Tori Kosara

Senior Editor Tori Kosara
Designers Stefan Georgiou and Thelma-Jane Robb
Jacket Designer Guy Harvey
Pre-production Producer Siu Yin Chan
Producer Lloyd Robertson
Design Manager Guy Harvey
Managing Editor Sarah Harland
Publisher Julie Ferris
Art Director Lisa Lanzarini
Publishing Director Simon Beecroft

Reading Consultant Maureen Fernandes

First published in Great Britain in 2019 by
Dorling Kindersley Limited
80 Strand, London WC2R 0RL
A Penguin Random House Company

10 9 8 7 6 5 4 3 2 1
001—314127—Feb/2019

ISBN: 978-0-24137-784-0

Printed and bound in China

www.dk.com
www.fingerlings.com

A WORLD OF IDEAS:
SEE ALL THERE IS TO KNOW

Contents

Meet the unicorns

The unicorns are Gigi, Alika, Gemma, Molly, Skye and Stella.

They have magical powers!

Alika

Gigi

Skye

Stella

Gemma

Molly

5

Sparkle Heights

The unicorns live in a town.
It is named Sparkle Heights.
Everything is made of sweets.
Yum!

Sweet home

There are so many sweet things to eat in Sparkle Heights.

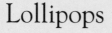
Lollipops

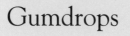
Gumdrops

Tarts

Candy floss
clouds

Sprinkles

Cake

Gigi

Gigi loves her friends.
She shares her magic
with them.
Gigi is a good friend.

Skye

Skye uses magic to fly.
She flies above the candy
floss clouds.
Zoom!

Stella

Stella looks at magic stars.
She makes wishes on them.
Her dreams come true!

Alika

Alika likes sparkles.
She leaves magic sparkles
wherever she goes.

Rainbow magic

Gemma and Molly look
for magic rainbows.
The colours are so pretty!

Gemma

Molly

Best friends

The unicorns are friends.
Friendship is the best magic!

Quiz

1. Where do the unicorns live?

2. What is everything in Sparkle Heights made of?

3. Who shares magic with her friends?

4. Which unicorn flies over clouds?

5. Which unicorns look for rainbows?

6. What is the best magic of all?